NIGHT ANIMALS

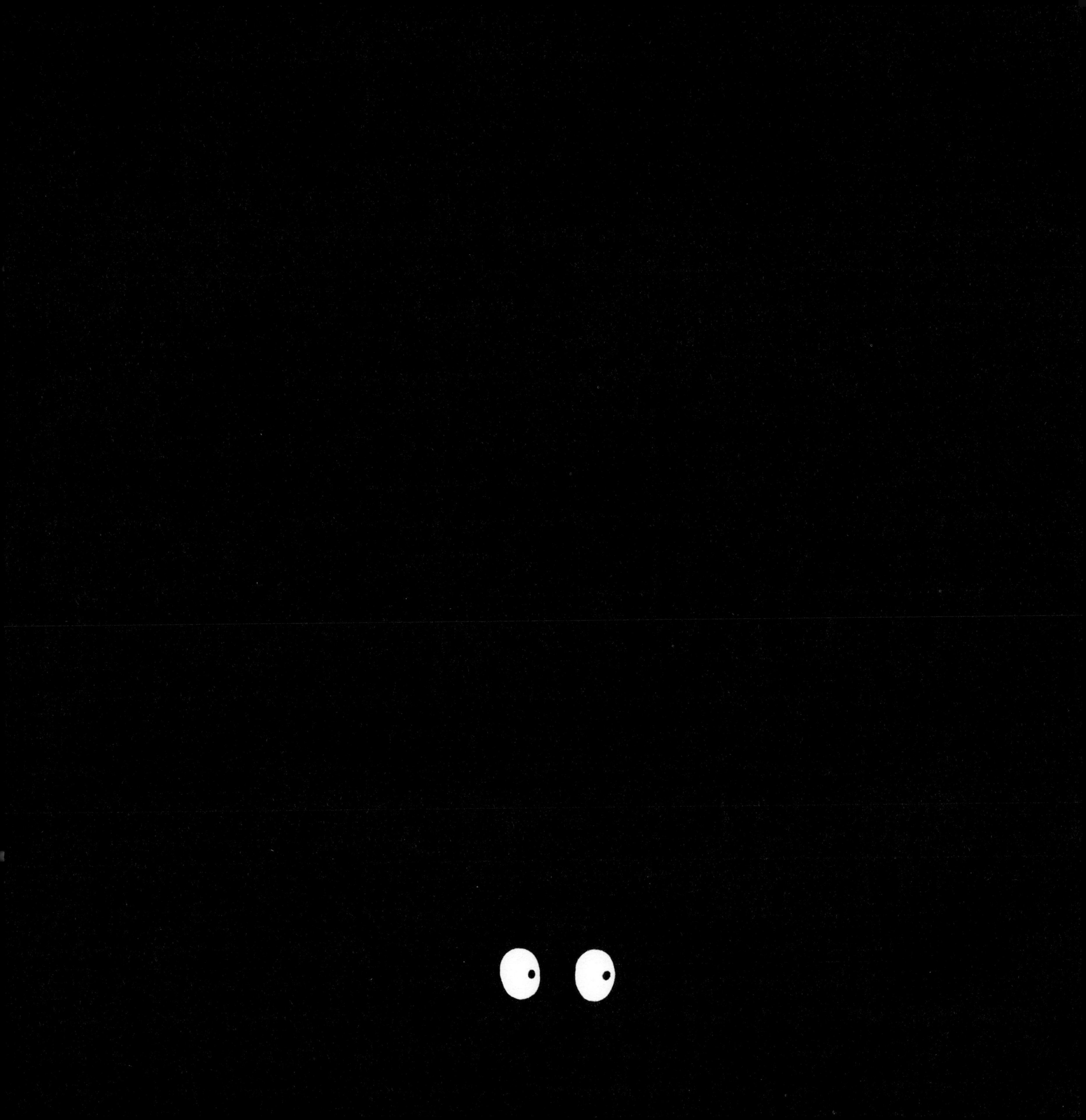

NIGHT ANIMALS

Gianna Marino

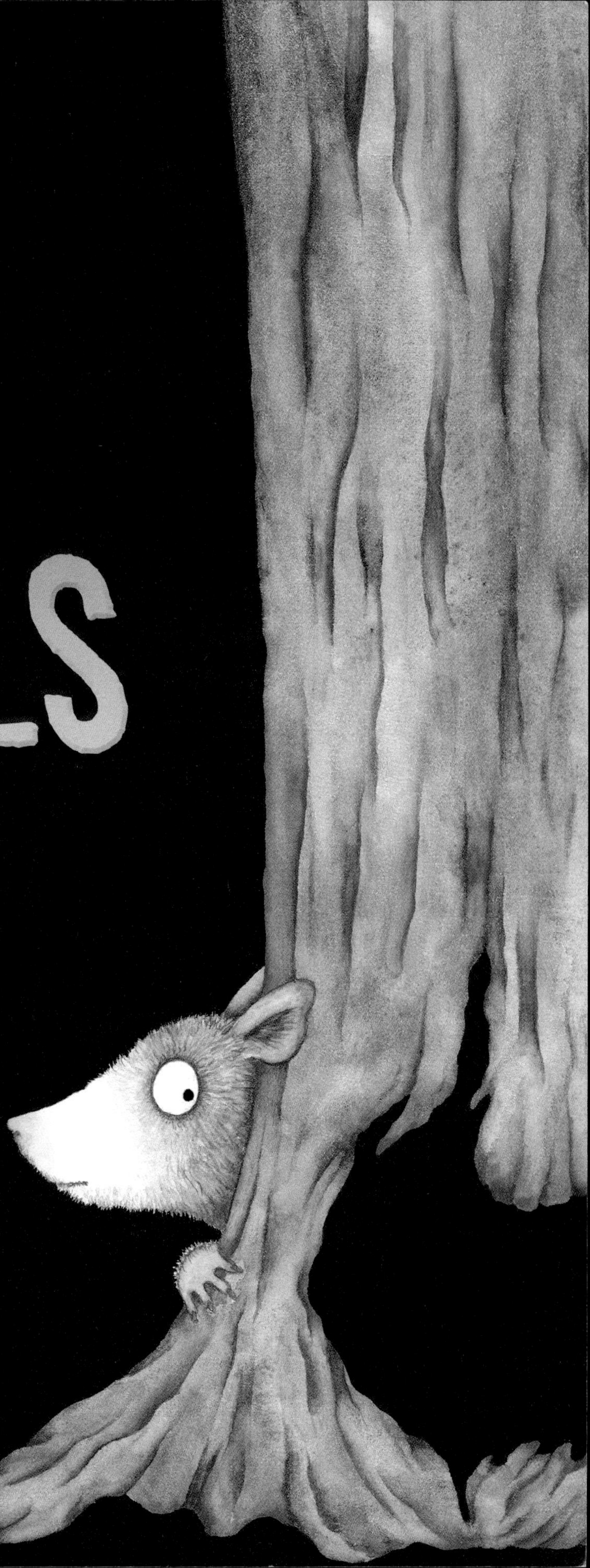

SCHOLASTIC INC.

Hey Possum, what are you doing in there?

I'm hiding!
Shhhhhh!!

What are we hiding from?

Night animals! Now keep QUIET!

Can you
move over?

Let's find somewhere else.
Sigh ...

rrrrrrrrroooooooo

Did you hear something?
Are you trying to scare me?

HELP ME!
Aaaarrrrooooooo

Help YOU!? You're a wolf!

But SOMETHING is following me!

What is it?

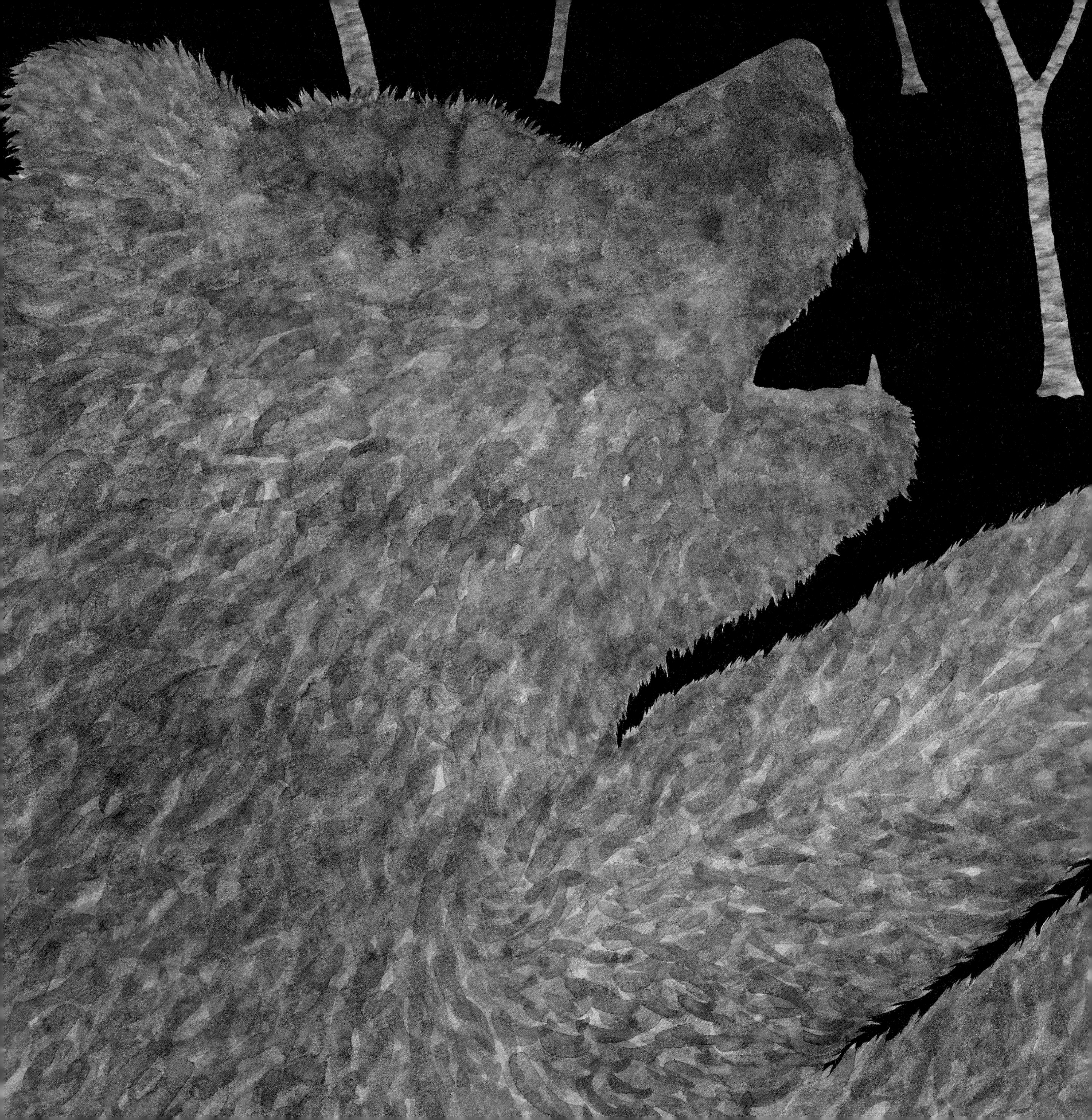

It's big and hairy with long, sharp claws!
I'm not here.

You guys gotta help me! Something HUGE is coming!

Why is the sky getting darker?
What can be bigger than a BEAR??

NIGHT ANIMAL!
RUN!

HIDE!

STOP!

What are you so scared of?

We're scared of night animals!

But you ARE night animals.

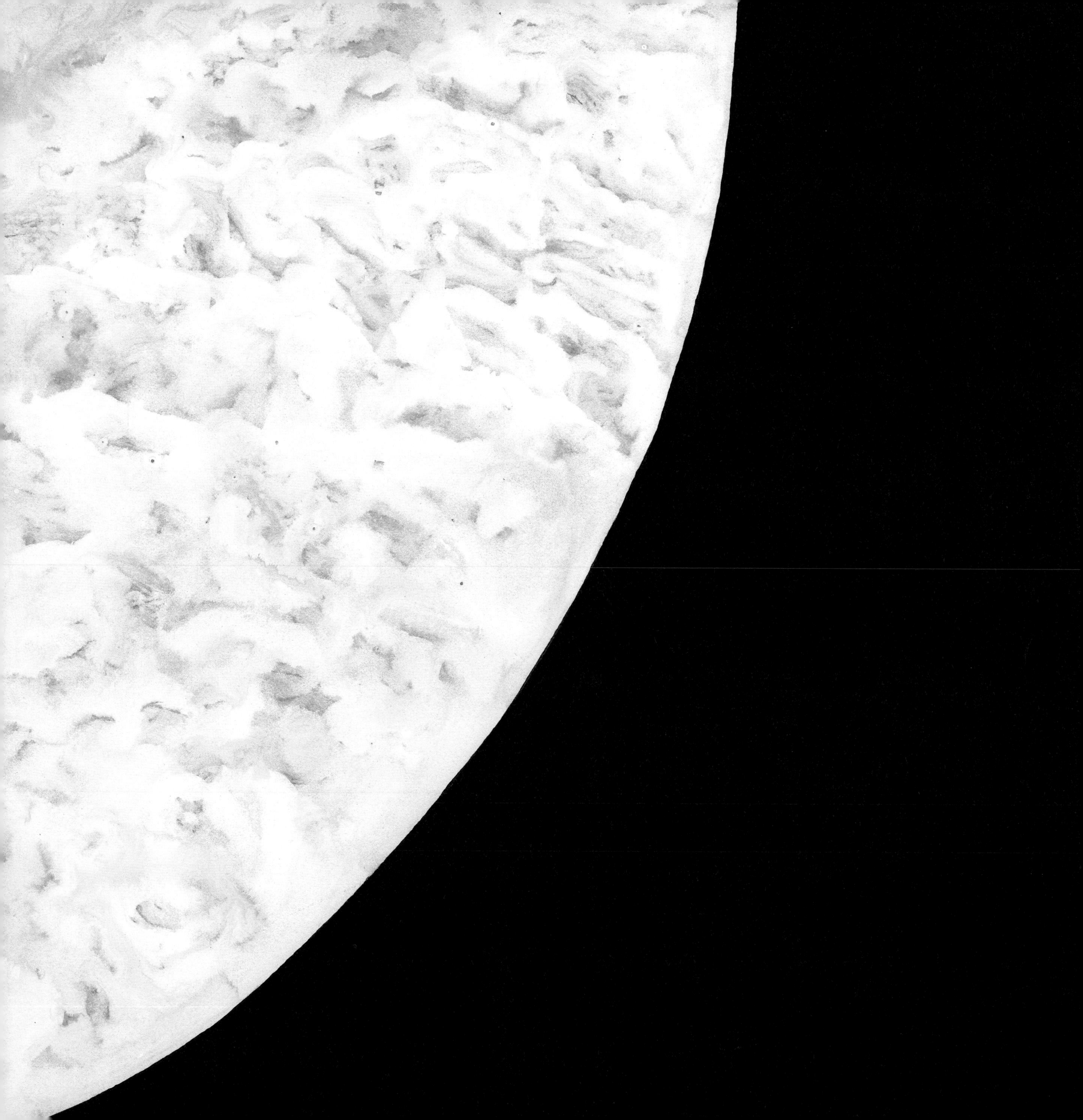

Ohhh

hhh
Did you hear something?

Click

RUN!
RUN!

RUN!

Hoo
Hoo
Hoo

For the Revisionaries—
Jim, Karen, Lynn, Maria, Arree, and Yuyi.
You make the dark a little less scary.

ISBN 978-1-338-10285-7

Published by Scholastic Inc., 557 Broadway, New York, NY 10012, by arrangement with Viking Children's Books, an imprint of Penguin Young Readers Group, a division of Penguin Random House LLC.

12 11 10 9 8 7 6 5 4 3 2 1 16 17 18 19 20 21

Printed in the U.S.A. 08

This edition first printing, September 2016

Designed by Nancy Brennan
The illustrations for this book were rendered in gouache and ink on Fabriano Artistico paper.